Fiction

Hey, Robin!

Robin took a deep breath. "I wish I was brave. I wish I was strong."

"Is that your true and only wish in this world?" asked Meg.

Robin nodded, and nodded again.

"Then listen to me," said Meg. "Your wish shall be granted. But first you must journey to the Blue Mountain and climb to the top. There you will find a spring of clear water. Fill the flask that I shall give you, and bring it back. Then you shall have your heart's desire. But do not take a drop for yourself, even if your lips burn with thrist. Be warned." And Robin did as he was told, as far as he was able. But it was a long time before he came to the Blue Mountain, and he forgot the old woman's instruction.

Other Young Lions Storybooks

ROBERT LEESON

Hey, Robin!

Illustrated by Helen Leetham

Young Lions
An Imprint of HarperCollinsPublishers

First published in Great Britain in 1989
by A & C Black (Publishers)
First published in Young Lions 1991
This impression 1993

Young Lions is an imprint of
HarperCollins Children's Books,
a division of HarperCollins Publishers Ltd,
77–85 Fulham Palace Road,
Hammersmith, London W6 8JB

Printed and bound in Great Britain by
HarperCollins Manufacturing, Glasgow

For Suzannah, Joanna and Simon

1

SNATCHING AND DODGING

Robin was born in a little town by a river. Across the river, to the east, lay the forest, dark and gloomy. To the west lay the broad plains, meadows and cornfields and farms. And, beyond them, rose the Blue Mountain, like a distant cloud.

In the middle of the town was the market place, with inns and stalls and the stocks where people were tied up and whipped, or pelted with rubbish – if they did something wrong, and they were caught.

The market place was Robin's home. He got his living there by day and slept under a stall by night. He had no parents, so there was just one in his family. Now, a family of one doesn't need much feeding. Which was just as well because there was not much to eat. All the same, Robin was often hungry.

On market days, people came in from the farms with wagon-loads of produce if they were well off, or with sacks, bundles and baskets on their shoulders if they were poor.

And what was left under the stalls at night, broken vegetables, bruised fruit, scraps of baked meat and salt fish, the heel of a loaf or a morsel of pastry, was food for a lad with a good appetite.

Sometimes in the bustle and noise of the day, when people pushed and shoved and shouted at one another, and poked at the goods on the stalls, a turnip, an apple, a crust, might accidentally fall. If you were in the right place at the right time you might catch it. And if the stall holder didn't bother, or didn't see, you might get a bite before it fell on the ground and got dirty.

But Robin was not the only one who got his daily bread this way. A crowd of boys, his age and older, were round the stalls like a flock of starlings. They swooped and snatched, scattered and flew when any bakers or fishmongers cursed them or threatened to beat them. They were fast because the rule of the market place was: Don't get caught.

Robin was youngest. He was as smart as a sparrow. His eye was sharp and his hand was

quick. It had to be because he was smallest of all.

Others who were bigger would watch him, and when he had some choice bit of food in his fingers they would follow and snatch it from him. "Share out," they would cry. But they didn't mean it, for they never shared theirs with him. Then it was "Finders keepers".

Robin tried to be sharper and quicker. With spotting and dashing, snatching and dodging, he got a living. But not much of one. He didn't grow much, neither up, down, nor sideways.

He was always the smallest, always the weakest. And even if he grew, the bigger boys grew even more.

He wished he were stronger. He wished he were braver. But he wasn't. And so it might have gone on.

But one day, something unexpected happened.

2

OLD MEG

Every so often Old Meg would come to the market and set up her stall selling ointments and pills for people's aches and pains.

No one knew when she would come. Early in the morning she would appear out of the dark forest across the river. Then she would wade across the ford, her back bent low under her great leather sack.

As she walked through the market place, men and women made way for her. No one spoke to Meg. No one liked her. But one and all, they feared her. They feared her grim face and her pointed chin. And they feared the great black cat with yellow eyes that walked behind her.

Many came to her stall and bought. For it was said Meg could cure any ill. She could even make a wart vanish from hand or face simply by saying words over it.

Some called her a wise woman. Some called her a herb woman. And some called her other names. But no one really knew Meg. No one had ever followed her and her cat across the river into the deep forest where she lived.

She came to market with her bag full and went

away with it empty. And she did not care what people said. Robin watched her come to market and sit with the big cat curled up on top of the stalls. She did not cry her wares but sat and waited until people asked to buy. None of the boys ever tried to touch what belonged to Meg while the cat sat and watched.

Robin was afraid of her, too. But he did not follow at a safe distance and call her names under his breath like the other boys. He watched her and wished that he were like her. For Meg looked people in the face and was afraid of no one, even when she did not have a friend in the world.

But she had enemies.

One day in the market, when Meg set up her stall, Robin heard a muttering in the crowd. The murmur grew. Men and women left what they were doing and gathered round. The boys ran quickly to see what would happen. There was excitement in the air.

Suddenly a woman's voice was heard.

"She's put the evil eye on my cow. It died last night. But Sunday it was right as rain." Drawing breath, she shouted:

"She's wicked. She's a witch."

"Swim her in the river, that'll tell," bawled a drunken voice. "If she floats, she's a witch. If she drowns, she's not."

"Yes, swim her," yelled more voices. And the crowd pressed forward again. Robin saw their faces, angry, ugly, full of hate. He slipped away and dodged under arms and legs to the wall behind Meg's stall.

For a few seconds the old woman faced the crowd. Then, slowly without hurrying she began to collect her pots and boxes together.

But one of the boys snatched. A box fell to the ground, scattering the pills around. Now the others joined in the sport, tipping her goods over, throwing them in the air.

Then men and women began to follow the boys.

14

They started to pull down the stall, plank by plank. Soon they were ready to lay hands on her.

3

THE CHASE

Meg's stall was soon cleared and broken to match-wood. So her tormentors began to shower her with cabbage stalks, rotten apples and offal from the butcher's bins. Still they did not dare come close to her as she stood, eyes sparking fire, back to the wall.

Unseen by the crowd, Robin crept along the wall, crouching low till he came near Meg. He reached out and tugged at the skirt of her dress. For a second she looked down at him.

"Come quick," he urged. "They will kill you. Come. I'll show you the way."

He did not wait for her answer but slid away,

bent double. Ten yards along the wall was an alley at the side of the inn stables, a narrow gap wide enough only for one.

Robin heard the crowd roar. Now Meg was at his side. A second later she had slipped into the alley and vanished. All to be seen in the gap was the pale-faced boy.

One of the lads was first to realise what had happened. He pointed at Robin.

"He let her go," yelled the lad. "Witch boy!"

"Witch boy," howled the others. Now, cheated

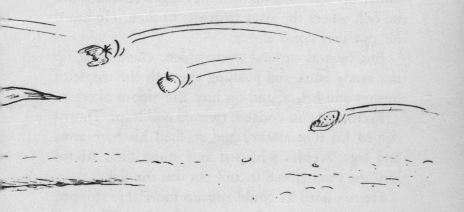

of their first sport, they began to pelt Robin with rubbish, followed by lumps of mud, and then stones.

Robin stood it as long as he could, arms over his bent head. Then he ducked into the alley and was away with the pack at his heels, running like the wind through side streets until he was clear of the town.

He ran faster than the others. They ran for fun. He ran for dear life. He ran alone. They ran in a crush and fell over one another as they stopped to snatch up stones. But still they came on behind him.

At the river bank he stopped, the breath burning in his chest. He looked back. Now most of the men and women had gone back to their stalls. But the lads and some idlers kept after him.

In front of him was the water. Beyond that the forest, like a dark wall. He had never dared go into it before. Now he did not dare stop.

He splashed through the ford, the spraying water under his feet soaking his old, ragged jerkin. Once he fell, where the river bed was broken. He heard his pursuers come closer.

But he was up and away again, clambering up the sandy bank and pushing through the tangle of bushes and briars, and on into the gloom of trees.

Robin ran and dodged, twisted and leapt. Thorns ripped his thin clothes and slashed his bare arms and legs. Nettles whipped and stung him. Above him the trees closed in and cut out the light.

He ran until he could run no more. He stopped and heard no more shouting behind him. The pack feared the wood more than he feared them. He was alone. He was lost.

There was no turning back now, though. Robin knew he could not return to the town. Worn out, he fell on to the moss and leaves and slept.

4

A LIGHT IN THE FOREST

Robin woke. He did not know if it were day or night, the trees were so thick. He did not know what to do, where to go. But if he stayed where he was he would perish of hunger. And he feared the creatures that lurked and rustled in the bushes.

He got to his feet and struggled on. The way before him was black as pitch. Roots and twining branches snatched at his arms and whipped his face. But he kept on because he did not dare to stay.

Then, out of the dark ahead of him, like the end of a tunnel, appeared a light. At first, it was as small as a pin. But as he struggled on, it began to glitter like a star. It grew and spread. Now it was a square of bright, warm glow.

At last he broke free of the trees and saw it was the window of a small cottage. Quietly, he crept forward round the corner and saw that the door was open, with light streaming out.

Inside the tiny kitchen the walls gleamed with brightly coloured plates and dishes. A fire leapt and sparked in the shining grate. In the middle of the floor stood a clean wooden table, without a cloth, but laid with bowls and a knife, bread and meat. One chair stood by the table and that was empty.

His mouth watered. His stomach rumbled. His hunger was painful. But he stood stock still on the doorstep as if he had been planted there.

The cottage was quiet. Somewhere a clock ticked. Was anyone there? He was very hungry, but he could not go in.

A woman's voice spoke, out of nowhere, soft, but clear.

"Why do you wait, Robin? Come in, sit down and eat."

Robin licked his lips.

"There is only a place for one."

"That one is you, Robin. Come. Eat."

Robin hesitated no longer. Swiftly he crossed the floor, sat down, rubbed his hands on his ragged clothes, and began to eat. He had never tasted such delicious bread and meat, so crusty, so tender. And the water in the cup that stood next to his plate was sweet and refreshing. Only when he had eaten did he look around him. And now his mouth opened in surprise. Over in the corner by the fire, was a rocking chair, moving gently to and fro.

In it sat a woman, dressed in a fine green robe. Her hair, pure white, was braided over her head. She sewed as she sat and watched him.

And in her lap sat a cat as black as coal, with eyes as yellow as the moon.

5

ROBIN'S WISH

"It is rude to stare, Robin," the woman chuckled, as she turned the cloth she was sewing.

But Robin could not help it. He stared because he knew the cat. It belonged to Old Meg. But he did not recognise the woman. She chuckled again.

"You do not know me. You thought the old baggage who peddled pills in the market could not look so fine as this."

Robin turned red and shook his head. But that was what he *was* thinking.

"What do you say, Robin? If those fools in the market place had seen me as I am now, would they have tried to throw me in the river?"

Robin slowly shook his head.

"But you, Robin," went on Meg, "you would not let them drown an old soul, even if she were ugly and dirty and wicked. Tell me, why did you help me?"

Robin thought about this and then he answered:

"Because you did not fear them. Even when you were pelted with rubbish, you faced them all. You did not take your eyes away from them. They were afraid of you." He took a deep breath. "I wish I was brave. I wish I was strong."

Old Meg put down her sewing and came over to Robin. She put a hand on his head.

"Is that your true and only wish in this world?"

Robin nodded, and nodded again.

"Then, listen to me," said Meg. "Your wish shall be granted. But first you must do something. You must journey to the Blue Mountain. You must climb to its top. There you will find a spring of clear water. Fill the flask that I shall give you and bring it back. Then you shall have your heart's desire.

"But," she warned. "Do not take the water for yourself. Do not drink a single drop, even if your lips burn with thirst. Do not drink. Remember what I tell you.

> *Happiness or pain*
> *Is for you to choose,*
> *When you give, you gain,*
> *When you take, you lose.*"

Gently Meg stroked Robin's head.

"Tomorrow," she whispered, "you shall set out. But now you shall sleep. Goodnight, Robin, and farewell."

6

OLD
MEG'S MAGIC

Robin woke. It was daylight, a fine spring morning.
Birds sang in the bushes and the sun shone in a clear
sky.

But he was alone. He lay on the grass at the
edge of the forest. The cottage was gone. Old Meg
was gone. The cat was gone. All had vanished like
a dream.

Was it a dream?

His stomach was full and comfortable. Now,
you can dream about food, but that does not fill
your stomach.

He sat up and looked at his hands and legs. They were clean. The scratches and cuts from briars and stones had all gone.

The old ragged jerkin had gone, too. In its place was a new one, well-fitting and warm. He touched the cloth. This was the coat Meg had been sewing. It could not be a dream.

Round his waist was a belt. And fastened to the belt was a bag. He opened it. Inside was a loaf of bread and a small leather bottle.

Now he knew for sure that it was no dream. For this was the flask he must take to the Blue Mountain and fill with water from the magic spring.

Magic? If this was no dream, if this were all true, then people were right about Meg. She was a witch and he had promised to do as she asked.

But, then, she had promised to grant his wish. And she had given him food and clothes. And never in his life had anyone given Robin anything.

So he thought no more of these things, but set out across the fields until he found a road that did not lead to the town. For he could not go back there again.

Now, which way should he go? There was only one answer to that question. He must go to the west, where the Blue Mountain lay like a cloud on the far horizon. How long would it take? He did not know. Maybe weeks, maybe months, maybe years.

How would he live? Summer was coming and he could gather berries. In autumn there would be nuts. But what would there be when winter came?

Robin thought no more of that. Winter must take its turn. He set off down the road and walked all that day. At night he slept under a hedge and woke shivering and cold, his clothes soaked in dew. But later the sun came out and dried and warmed and cheered him.

At night he ate from the loaf Meg had given him. It was tasty and crusty and filled his stomach. He kept back a small piece for the next day.

And strangely, next morning, when he awoke, he found a whole loaf in his wallet. So he did not go hungry. He walked always with the sun, towards the west. The days went by and the spring journeyed with him, towards the summer.

7

THE
LAST CRUST

Robin travelled on. The days grew longer and lighter as he walked. He rose with the sun as it stood up over the Dark Forest behind him to the east. He journeyed on with the sun above him until it set behind the Blue Mountain in the west. Then the dark, which had followed, caught up with him and he looked for a place to shelter for the night.

Sometimes, he was lucky and found a warm place in a little barn, bedding down among the hay. Sometimes, he was very lucky and the farmer's wife gave him a cup of milk fresh from the cow, while he chopped wood for her fire.

Sometimes he was unlucky and they shut the door in his face. "Clear off, vagabond. Move on," they shouted.

And sometimes, he was very unlucky and they set the dogs on him. He was chased, panting up the road. If he had not been quick-footed he would have felt their teeth in his legs.

He learnt a good deal as he moved on from day to day. He learnt about people and he learnt about dogs. If he tried to slip past quietly, out the hounds would come, lips curled back, teeth showing, making the air ring with their racket.

No matter how wide he walked past the farm gate, they would follow him. They had a nose for fear.

He found a branch, blown from a tree. When he had stripped the leaves and the twigs from it, he had a fine club. When he walked past a farm gate, he went with a bold step and swung his stick and whistled – even if he trembled a little inside. And the dogs sat on their haunches and growled but let him pass.

Days passed. Spring is a time of hope. But it is not a time of plenty. Little grows in the fields and woods to eat. Robin might have starved but for the bread Meg had given him.

Each night as he lay down, in the hay or behind a wall, or under a bush, he ate from the loaf. Then, before he slept, he stowed away the last crust.

And each morning when he woke and stretched himself, he looked inside the pouch on his belt. There, crisp and fresh as if it had just come from the baker's oven, was a new loaf. Thanks to Meg, he never quite went hungry.

But, one night, as he made his bed ready under a hedgerow, he was joined by a travelling companion.

It was a tall man in a ragged cloak. He carried a long staff bound with brass rings. His face was red and rough, his eyes were quick and blue and little tufts of white hair stood up from his wrinkled head.

"Well met, brother," he greeted Robin. "Can I sleep here? Two's company. It's lonely on the road sometimes."

Robin nodded. Why should he say no? The tramp sat down and began to talk. He talked until the sun had vanished, making Robin stare and smile with his tales of the wandering life.

Then he said, "Hey, brother. I'm starving. Have

you anything in that pouch of yours?"

Robin could not say no. He took out his last crust. What could he do? He had eaten, the man had not. He could not say, "I'm keeping this for myself."

He remembered Meg's words:

When you give, you gain,
When you take, you lose.

He gave the crust to his companion, who ate it in three big bites. Then he bid Robin goodnight, turned his back and was soon snoring.

8

WHEN YOU GIVE, YOU GAIN

Robin woke at daybreak. The air was crisp with late spring frost. His body was stiff with cold. He looked around and saw that he was alone. The wanderer had gone.

Robin put a hand to the pouch on his belt and opened it as he did each morning. But this time, there was no crisp new loaf sitting there. The pouch was empty.

His last crust had gone in the belly of his story-telling companion. The tramp had gone and not even said a word of farewell.

For a moment, Robin was angry. He did not expect a gift in return for his crust. It wasn't much to the tramp, though it meant a great deal to Robin. But a word of cheer before leaving, at least.

Then he shrugged his shoulders, and stretched his arms and legs. Next time, he would remember and be more careful. The rule of the road must be the same as the rule of the market place: Take what you can and give as little as you must.

It was very hard to go by Old Meg's words:

When you give, you gain,
When you take, you lose.

Still, he must be on his way. No good sitting there, grumbling to himself. He got to his feet to move on. But as he did, he stopped. Something made him stop. Not a sight, not a sound, but a faint smell. Just a whiff. But it made his eyes open wide.

It was a mixture of wood smoke and food frying. And with it there came the sound of crackling, and hissing, as if fat was spilling on to hot wood.

His stomach rumbled like a kettledrum. His mouth watered. He looked around. But there was nothing to be seen, though his nose and ears both told him, *Food*.

A voice called from the other side of the oak tree he had slept under.

"Hey, Robin. Hey, little brother. Still asleep? Don't let the world go by. Come and eat."

Robin jumped. It was the wanderer calling. He ran like a rabbit all the way round the tree's great trunk.

There, on a bare patch of earth, burned a fire, the sticks blazing and glowing, white wisps of smoke rising in the air. Over the embers, fixed on twigs, two fish were frying.

By the side of the fire sat the tramp, whistling to himself and slowly turning the fish. With each turn, the juice spat on the glowing wood and the smell wafted up with the smoke.

Robin's mouth opened wide again.

"Where . . ?"

The traveller nodded to the edge of the little wood.

"There's a stream down there. And under the stones the fish are half asleep in the cold. I was too quick for them. Or they were too slow for me. So, now they are our breakfast."

He looked at Robin.

"What, lad? Why do you stare? Do you think – did you truly think I would go off and leave you without a solitary word? Why, when you had given me your last crust?

"No, may I be struck dead on the spot if I should do such a thing. Such is not the rule of the road."

He reached out a hand and pushed Robin down.

"Come, eat. Then let's be on our way."

9

LONG JACK

Robin and the wayfarer, whose name was Long Jack, ate their fill, then went their way after Jack had scattered earth over the ashes of the fire and stamped it down.

As they walked, they talked together. Long Jack asked Robin where he was heading for and Robin told him. The tramp's eyes grew round.

"Why, Robin, you must be a bold little fellow to go up there. There's nothing but rocks and ghosts and trolls."

"Still, I have said I will go and bring back water from the spring," answered Robin.

"Suit yourself. See, I'll go with you some of the way, for I'm headed for the west myself."

So they travelled together. And it was a good time for Robin. He was never hungry while he tramped with Long Jack.

The wanderer taught him how to raise fish with his bare hands from under the banks of streams, lying still so as not to cast a shadow on the water. He taught him how to set snares of twine for rabbits, and throw stones with a sling as true as any arrow. Robin learnt well and fast, for his eye was clear and his mind was quick.

The summer months went by. Corn grew yellow and bright flowers bloomed in the meadows. On the farms people began to be busy with the harvest.

Long Jack watched the men and women in the fields and he chuckled.

"Such hard work," he said, "is good for those who stand still and want a roof over their heads. But not for those who travel on."

He took care to call at farms only when the sun was setting. Then, as folk came in from the fields and gathered in the kitchens and the barns, Long Jack would step up to the door, tug with his fingers on his white curls and greet the farmer's wife with great respect.

Robin and he would be welcomed in to share the meal. And after everyone had eaten they would turn to Jack and call for a story.

Long Jack never failed. He had a different tale for every farm. He would keep an eye on his listeners as he talked, to be sure he pleased them. And he always did.

But Long Jack did not call at every farm. He knew each farmer well and knew where he would be welcome, and where not. He showed Robin marks carved in trees and on gateposts, marks left by others on the road. Here was a good place to stop. Here they would chase you away.

At last harvest time was over. Leaves in the woods began to turn yellow and red, and in the field the corn stubble blazed and smoked as it was burnt off.

One day Long Jack said, "Robin, lad. It gets colder. Winter's coming. I shall go where I can find more warmth and shelter. We must part company, if you will go to the Blue Mountain."

"I must go," said Robin.

"Then, at the next crossroads, you go to the left and I to the right. You go uphill, I go down."

When they came to where the ways parted, Long Jack took Robin's hand.

"Go well, little Robin. And, if you ever need a friend, Long Jack's your man."

They parted company then. Robin set off uphill and Long Jack went down.

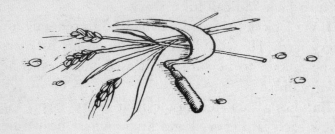

ROCKS AND MIST AND TROLLS!

When the harvest work was over and done, Robin said goodbye to the farm people. He left the country lanes and began to climb the hill tracks.

At first he climbed through woods where falling leaves covered the ground like a soft mat. Amid the dark tree branches the birch with its silver trunk and red leaves shone like a beacon fire.

Day by day he climbed. He ate berries and nuts for food. He drank from streams that trickled down the hillside. At night he slept on the leaves under the trees. The sky was full of stars and the air was still warm.

He was higher above the valley now and getting farther from farms and cottages. He met no one and he thought nothing of this for he was used to his own company.

But he was not alone.

Sometimes in the evening, when shadows lengthened through the trees, he heard quick footsteps in the bushes. Something was moving along beside him, always out of sight, but never far away. When he lay down to sleep he put his stick and his sling with round pebbles close to his hand.

Once, twice in the night, he woke, to see two

eyes like golden fire in the deep dark. For a moment they watched him. Then quickly, without noise, they were gone. And after that he saw and heard no more of the unseen creature.

Day by day he climbed, and at last came clear of the wood. Now the hill slopes stretched up before him. First, short green turf where sheep grazed, next stone walls, then brown bracken and rough boulders.

And above and beyond, the rock slopes towered up to the peak, blue grey against the autumn sky. He was near the end of his journey. For this was the Blue Mountain.

Now he was away from the woods, the wind grew cold. Mornings were misty and the water in rock pools was cold. One evening he came across a shepherds' hut. It was no more than a stone shelter with a turf roof. But a fire blazed in front of the door and two shepherds sat over their supper.

They greeted him, and shared their stew with him, while he told them of his journey. But why was he on the mountain, they wanted to know.

"There's nothing up there but rocks and mist and trolls," said one.

"I shall not wait to see them," answered Robin. "I shall fill my flask from the spring at the mountain peak, then come down again as quick as I may."

They looked at one another, then said:

"There is one thing to beware of."

"What is that?"

The older shepherd poked the fire.

"There is a great creature that kills our sheep. We have never come near it and do not know if it is a wolf or what."

"But it does not eat them," said the other. "It only tears at them and kills them."

He shivered.

"I say it's no beast. It is the Evil One."

At last they lay down to rest. But they did not let the fire go out all through the night.

11

DO NOT DRINK

Next day when the air was chill and white with mist, Robin said goodbye to his friends the shepherds.

"Do not linger on the Blue Mountain," they warned him.

Robin shook his head. He did not need to be told. The mountain loomed above him in the mist, cold and menacing.

As he climbed through the morning, the mist blew away. The sky was hard and clear above and the sun shone full on him as he clambered from rock to rock, or slithered over the loose shale.

Soon he began to sweat. But he did not stop to rest, though his legs and arms ached and his mouth was dry. He did not dare to pass a night on that bare mountain peak, but must reach it and return before nightfall.

When the sun stood high, he came to the mountain summit where a huge boulder, square as a house, balanced on the very point. And beneath it he saw the magic spring bubbling up and running away with a tinkling sound in the still air.

His mouth was like sand and his throat seemed on fire. Without a thought he fell on his knees and drank quickly. The water was like wine on his lips. He had quite forgotten Meg's words, *Do not drink.*

In that moment, the spring, the great rock, the mountain itself vanished. He fell twisting and turning. All was dark around him. When he opened his eyes, he lay on the grass by the stone shelter. The two shepherds looked down on him in amazement. It was already sunset.

They asked him no questions, and let him spend that night in their hut. But in the morning the old shepherd said:

"Hey, Robin. Leave this foolishness. Stay here with us. We can use another hand with the flocks."

But Robin did not listen. Once again he set out in the morning mists. Once again the mists cleared. The sun warmed his tired limbs and parched his throat. And again near noon he stood by the hanging rock.

This time he remembered Old Meg's words. His thirst was terrible but he did not take the water to drink.

He bent down and filled the flask from his pouch. But as he did this his hand brushed the water. And without thinking he licked the drops from his fingers.

Yet again, the rock and the spring vanished from view and he felt himself fall down and down. This time he woke on the bare mountain slope. And it was still afternoon, though the sun was moving down the western sky. But the flask at his belt was empty.

Now he picked himself up and climbed again. His legs and arms felt as heavy as lead and each step was an effort. But his fear of being benighted on the Blue Mountain was greater than his weariness.

In the early evening, when the eastern side of the hanging rock was gloomy, he came for the third time to the magic spring.

This time, with great care, he filled the flask. Not one drop of water touched his fingers. He stood up, fastened the flask into his pouch, and went down the mountain once more.

But now his tiredness seemed to drop away. He moved with a sure foot from rock to rock and whistled as he went.

As the sun was going down he came back to the mountain pastures. Just below he could see the sheep flocks, white against the shadowy green. And there was the shepherds' hut with smoke rising from the fire.

But something was wrong. Terribly wrong.

12

THREE STONES AND
A SLING

In the meadow below Robin, the sheep were scattering, running and tumbling. Their terrified cries split the evening air.

Right among them like a giant shadow was a black beast, pointed head and ears, cruel white teeth shining against the fur. It was a cat, but a cat like no one had ever seen or dreamt of. Huge, long and powerful, it sprang upon the sheep as they ran to and fro.

First one was struck down. The great cat did not stop to feed but threw itself on another victim and another.

Robin heard men shout. He saw the shepherds, sticks in hand, run bravely but desperately from their hut.

For a moment he was held still by terror, as if his feet had grown roots in the grass. Then he saw the terrible cat swing from the killed sheep and spring towards the shepherds.

Brave as they were, they turned and fled. The older man stumbled and fell full on the ground as the cat drew its length together to leap upon his back.

Life rushed back into Robin's arms and legs.

He let out a great shout that sounded above the bleating of the sheep and the snarling of the cat.

In that instant it turned from its death leap on the fallen shepherd. Swerving in the air, and away from its prey, it now bounded forward, clearing the pasture wall and heading straight for Robin.

He saw it come on. Its yellow eyes, meeting the rays of the sun low in the sky, flashed fire.

Robin drew his sling from the loop on his belt,
and from the pouch where the flask with the magic
water lay, three stones, round and smooth, which
he had taken from the brook the other day.

Now he waited as the cat came closer with
every stretch of its mighty legs.

Then, at the moment of his choice, as the wanderer had taught him, he swung the thongs of his
sling, once, twice, three times.

The last stone struck as the cat was no more
than ten feet away. Its strength failed at the last
moment, but its final leap carried it to Robin's
feet, where it lay still, its head resting against his
leg.

13

A CAT LIKE
NO OTHER CAT

Robin dropped down on his knees by the body
of the cat as it lay on the grass. Now it seemed
smaller. The fur which had stood up like spikes
lay smooth on its head and back.

A shadow passed over him. He looked up to
see the younger shepherd, staff raised to bring it
down full force on the cat's skull.

"Wait," shouted Robin.

"What? Can't you see?" the man answered, pale
and angry. "It lives. See the breath is still in it."

So it was. Its side rose and fell gently as if the
wild cat slept. Robin raised a hand and pushed the
staff aside. For he had seen something the shepherd
had not.

Slowly he lifted the beast's head and pulled
apart its jaws with their savage teeth. The shepherd
stared.

"Why, look now," he said.

Wedged into the roof of the mouth, across the
throat, was a jagged bone. The cat had been in a
desperate rage of hunger, ready to kill but not able
to eat.

Propping open the jaws with a stick, Robin
thrust in his hand and wrestled the bone from

the cat's mouth. Then he let the jaws close and the animal slept on.

The old shepherd came up and stood looking down at the cat.

"Still, we must kill it," he said. And the younger shepherd nodded.

Robin shook his head.

"I will not let you kill the cat," he said. They heard his voice and said no more, but went to gather their flocks together.

Robin took a rope and bound the cat's fore and hind legs together. That night it lay outside the hut, still and quiet. But the sheep were afraid and bleated in the dark and the men did not sleep.

In the morning they said to Robin:

"See, Robin. We are grateful to you. You saved our lives and our flocks. But you cannot stay with the cat, not here."

And the younger one added, "That is no wild cat. That is the Evil One."

"Robin, lad," said the older man. "We would gladly have you stay. But not the cat. If you will keep it by you, then you must leave us. You must go from here."

Robin nodded.

"I will go. I have done what I came to do and now I must go back to the place where I was born."

The shepherds shook their heads and said:

"You will go back there? You told us that they

47

drove you out."

"Yes," answered Robin. "Back I must go, and finish my task."

That next day, Robin got up with the dawn. He looped the rope round the cat's neck, unfastened its legs and marched away through the forests where all the leaves had fallen and the trees were now bare.

When he was out of sight of the pasture, he took the rope from the cat's neck. He knew that if it chose to escape he could not hold it. And he did not need to hold it, for the cat ran silently by his side.

As they passed by the farms, the dogs did not bark, but crawled away and whimpered as they smelt the cat. As they passed the cottages, the mothers took their children indoors at the sight of the lean and sunburnt lad with the great yellow-eyed cat at his heels.

"There's a fearless rogue," said the farmers on their carts as Robin passed them in the lanes. No one stopped him. All made way for him. But no one fade him enter and eat bread or drink a cup of milk.

And he paid no heed, but marched on with the cat at his side until the day when he saw once more the town by the river in the shadow of the Dark Forest – the place where he was born.

14

ROBIN'S RETURN

Down on the plain, away from the hills, there was still autumn in the air. There were berries on the bush and the sun was gentle and warm.

But Robin did not linger on the country lanes as he had done in the summer. Those days were gone. He strode swiftly, the big cat at his side. No one stopped him. No one held him back. No one said *Good Day* and he spoke to no one.

When October was half gone, he came back to his home town in the middle of the day when the market square was crowded and noisy with buying and selling.

The dogs were first to see him come. They ran out, growling and barking. But when they saw the cat, their hair rose up on their necks, their growls changed to whimpers and they slunk back, tails between legs, underneath the stalls.

Next, the boys saw Robin. At first they did not know him. His face and arms were deep burnt by the sun, his clothes were dusty. He had grown taller, leaner. He walked with a firm tread and swung his stick as he walked.

Then they knew him.

"Hey, look who comes," they called. People in

the crowd began to stop what they were doing, to turn and stare.

"See, it's the witch boy, come back to defy us," they shouted. "Let's thrash him. Let's finish what we started last time."

They began to take up things to throw. But as they did, they stopped. They hesitated and they looked, and looked again.

Now they saw the cat lope by his side, head swinging, yellow eyes gleaming. And now they let their stones and rubbish fall from their hands. They halted in their stride and some began to turn away.

A woman screamed:

"The witch boy's back and brought Old Nick

with him."

That was enough. The market crowd began to shift like a pot coming to the boil. Some turned this way, others that. Some pushed to see, some to get away. And the more they pushed and the more they saw, the more they panicked.

Soon the whole crowd was on the go, with yells and shrieks as they understood what was going on. Now everyone moved one way – away from the dusty ragged traveller and his fearsome companion.

Stalls were pushed over and broken, fruit and vegetables flew in the air and rolled in the dust. People tripped and fell as they ran. The whole market square was in pandemonium.

And first to run away were the boys who had chased and pelted Old Meg and Robin in the spring. They shoved and fell over each other. And the biggest were the first away.

As the crowd ran, Robin laughed. And his laughter seemed to put more fear into them. He snatched up rubbish from the ground and pelted his old foes as they fled away.

He laughed still when the market place was empty and the soldiers came with pike and drum to seize him. They took him by force. There were ten of them and still they were afraid.

They marched him through the empty streets and threw him in the jail. But they did not take the cat because the cat had gone. It had vanished clean away.

15

JAILED

Robin lay in the jail for seven days, with straw for his bed, stale bread and foul water for his food and drink.

Then they took him to the Guildhall where the Mayor sat in his red robe and white fur, in a chair on a high platform.

The Mayor looked down his long nose at Robin.

"What is his crime?" he asked the Beadle in his green coat with brass buttons.

"Terrible crimes," huffed the Beadle and read from a scroll.

"One. He rescued a witch from trial by water."

"I saved an old woman from drowning," said Robin.

"Shut your mouth, rogue," answered the Mayor.

"Two," puffed the Beadle. "He caused a riot to let the witch escape."

"They caused the riot," said Robin.

"Shut your mouth, rogue," answered the Mayor.

"Three," boomed the Beadle, raising his voice to stop Robin speaking again. "He left the town without permission.

"Four. He came back with a monstrous creature, a servant of the Devil, to menace the peaceful folk

52

of this town.

"Five. He caused a riot. He destroyed the stalls and goods of honest market men and women. A troop of soldiers was needed to put it down."

The Mayor's face was grim. He looked down his long nose at Robin.

"Now, fellow, what do you say?"

"It was not a Devil's creature. It was a cat from the hills. It touched no one."

"And where is this harmless cat?" asked the Mayor with a sneer.

"I do not know," said Robin.

"It vanished clean away when its evil work was done," said the Beadle.

"I have done no wrong," Robin started to say. But the Mayor spoke louder.

"Enough, enough. You are guilty, five times. Everyone knows you are guilty and that is enough. Witchcraft, rioting, helping the Evil One. Prison is not enough. Flogging is not enough. Hanging is the only fit punishment."

The Mayor thought for a moment and stroked his chin.

"In seven days' time it is All Hallows' Eve. The town will be full of folk from far and wide. We will make an example of you that will not be forgotten.

"Take him back to the jail and guard him well. And on the day fixed, he shall be taken out in the market place to be hanged where all can see him." '

16

A VOICE IN
THE DARK

All Hallows' Eve came nearer, and the town began
to be crowded with people who journeyed in from
farms and villages even as far as the distant hills.
The market square was full every day with those
who bought and sold, to make ready for the cold
winter.

Robin heard them as they shouted to one another.
He heard them singing and drinking in the taverns.
And more than once he heard people talking under
his jail window. He heard the boys say to one
another:

"Robin's in there."

"Not for long."

"Tomorrow he'll come out."

"And they'll hang him."

"What if he escapes?"

"He's guarded night and day."

All the same, that day, before sunset, the guards
came and took Robin from the jail and marched
him to the castle over the market place. They put
him in the deepest cell below the walls. It was so
dark he could not see his hands before his face.

He lay in the night and listened to the rustling
of the rats and thought about all that had happened

in his life. And tomorrow it would end.

While he was thinking, he heard a noise in the straw that was louder than the rustling of rats.

"Good sir," said a feeble voice, like the crackling of a dry leaf.

"Who calls?" asked Robin. "I cannot see you."

"Five paces to your right," came the whisper. "I cannot move."

Robin moved five paces and in the dark he felt someone lying in the straw, frail and old, clothed in dirty rags. He could not say if it was man or woman.

"I am dying," said the voice, so low, Robin could barely hear it. "My throat's on fire. Give me something to drink. Do not let me die in torment."

"What can I give you?" asked Robin. "They left me neither bread nor water."

"Ah, my throat burns so," muttered the weak voice. "Can you not help me? Will you not help me?"

Robin thought. And he remembered that in his pouch lay the flask with the water from the Magic Spring. He had travelled far and risked much to get and bring it back.

Should he give it now to someone who would not live beyond the next day? Was all his journey just for that?

Ah, well, he thought. I shall not live beyond tomorrow.

So he took the flask and held it to the parched old lips. In a moment the precious magic water was all gone.

"Bless you, sir," said the voice. And did not speak again. All was silent in the cell now. Even the rats were still.

Robin lay on the straw and watched the grey light of dawn come through the bars of the tiny window.

He thought about all that he had seen and done. He thought about his journey to the Blue Mountain and why he had gone. He thought about Meg's words.

> *Happiness or pain*
> *Is for you to choose,*
> *When you give, you gain,*
> *When you take, you lose.*

What did it mean? He did not know. And what did it matter? Today it was all to end.

He thought about that. And he was not afraid.

17

TO THE GALLOWS

That day, as the sun showed above the Dark Forest, across the river, the guards took Robin from the castle prison. In the guard room they gave him bread and meat.

Robin asked them, "Who was that poor old soul who shared my cell last night?"

They stared at him and laughed.

"Old soul? What old soul? You had no one with you. When they're going to hang you, you get a room of your own for your last sleep."

Robin opened his pouch and took out the flask. It was empty. He put it carefully back.

"Why did you do that?" asked the guard.

"I may need it," said Robin.

They laughed.

"Aye, where you're going you'll need that, witch boy."

Robin looked at them calmly and they were silent.

Outside it was cold. A chill wind blew from the east.

"Soon be snow," said the guards as they put Robin in a cart. They whipped up the horse, and the cart rolled over the drawbridge and down the cobbled street to the market place.

The street was crowded, and down below them the market place was packed. The stalls had been taken down to make room for the people. But in the middle of the square stood the gallows platform, with the rope hanging down.

There was no shouting. But the murmur of the crowd was like the sea. Men and women muttered to each other.

"There goes the witch boy."

The cart rolled on more slowly. Halfway down the hill someone shouted above the murmuring of the crowd.

"Hey, Robin!"

Robin turned. Just a yard or two away, he saw a familiar weatherbeaten face, with spikes of white hair above. It was Long Jack, the wanderer.

"What? Will they hang you, Robin?"

Robin nodded and Long Jack called out:

"Why, it's a shame to hang a good lad."

Some in the crowd nodded and said, "Yes, true". But others answered, "No, he's the witch boy". And people began to push each other. The soldiers grew afraid and urged on the horse as the crowd grew thicker.

At the corner of the market square someone called again:

"Hey, Robin!"

He saw in the crowd two farmers he had worked for.

"What, Robin, will they hang you?"

Robin nodded and they said:

"Why, that's a sin."

The crowd jostled even more. People were shouting now and shoving so much that the cart came to a halt in the market place in front of the inn. Then more voices called:

"Hey, Robin."

Just a yard or two away were shepherds down from the hills, skin jackets on their shoulders and sticks in their hands.

"It's a crime to hang a good lad," they shouted. "We'll not see it done." And they began to lay about Robin's tormenters with their sticks and in a moment the great crowd was in turmoil.

Now Long Jack appeared at the side of the cart, knife in hand. He dived beneath the horse's belly. The cart shook and tilted down as the harness was cut. The guard beside Robin was thrown off his

feet and as quick as a cat Robin jumped from the cart and into the crowd. Hands snatched at him, but they were beaten off by the shepherds' sticks.

A way opened before Robin and he saw again the narrow lane down which he had run with Old Meg in the spring. He dived into the alley and ran like the wind with the shouts of his pursuers behind him. He ran through the streets beyond, out across the meadow and on towards the Dark Forest.

The river was in flood, but he did not hold back. He rushed into the current and, walking and swimming, he struggled through the brown water.

On the other side, the trees were gaunt and bare, the leaves falling down like rain in the biting wind. Snow fell with the leaves.

On ran Robin, his foes far behind. He was leaving his home town for the last time. He was free.

18

ESCAPE

Robin tramped all day through the forest. Beneath his feet, dead bushes and briars crackled as he walked. The sky was grey above and the trees began to whiten in the snow.

He was no longer in danger, but he did not stop. On he went as the sky above grew darker until he could hardly see a foot before him.

Then, when night came, he saw again a light in the distance. First like the point of a pin, then like a star, and at last like a square of window.

There again was the clearing among the trees. There was the tiny square cottage with the lamp burning. The door stood open, and the table was laid for supper. He stood a moment at the door till a woman's voice said:

"Why do you wait, Robin? Come and eat."

He entered and sat down at the table and began to eat. A fire burned in the grate. In front of the fire lay the cat, looking at Robin with its yellow eyes. And beyond the fire, in her rocking chair, sat Old Meg in her green gown, stitching away at a cloth which she held across her lap.

When Robin had finished eating, Meg put down her sewing.

"Well, Robin. You have had a long journey. I see your clothes are worn and ragged. You are taller and your face is brown with the sun."

Robin nodded. And the old woman went on:

"Have you done what you set out to do? Have you brought back the water from the Blue Mountain for me?"

Robin was silent.

Old Meg smiled. "Have you forgotten?"

He shook his head. "No. I did go to the Blue Mountain. I kept my promise."

"Where is the water, then?"

Robin held up the bottle from his pouch.

"It is empty, Meg. I gave the water to an old

soul dying in prison."

"What?" said Meg. "You gave it to someone dying? What did they need it for?"

Robin shrugged.

"I do not know. But their need was very great. So I gave it."

Meg put down her sewing and stood by Robin. She put a hand on his head.

> *Happiness or pain*
> *Is for you to choose,*
> *When you give, you gain,*
> *When you take, you lose.*

She stroked Robin's head.

"You have done well, Robin. You kept your promise. And I have kept mine."

"Your promise?" asked Robin.

"I promised that you should find courage and you have."

And that was true.

Old Meg stroked Robin's hair again and now he felt he would go to sleep for a long time.

"Tomorrow you will start your journey again. Leave this land and travel south to the mountains where no one goes for fear of giants.

"When you come through the mountains, go with the sun to your journey's end."

"How will I know where the journey ends?" asked Robin, half asleep.

"You will know," said Meg.

19

JOURNEY'S END

Robin woke with the dawn. He lay on the ground beyond the forest. All was white with snow. He looked round and stretched his arms and legs. They were washed and clean and his old, ragged jerkin had gone. In its place was a new one, fine and warm. By his side lay a long staff bound with brass rings.

He stood up. The sun shone pale on the skyline. Turning to face the south, he set out along the edge of the forest and tramped until he left it far behind.

Day by day he journeyed, always keeping the sun on his left hand in the morning and on his right hand when afternoon and evening came.

He sheltered in the farms and got food from the farmers. Sometimes he worked for them, feeding the cattle and cutting logs. And when there was no work to do he sat in the evening in the kitchen and told tales. He told all the stories he had heard from Long Jack. And when they were done he told stories of his own.

But none was listened to more eagerly, by young and old, than the story of how Robin journeyed to the Blue Mountain in search of the magic water and how he came back and what was done to him in the town where he was born.

"Stay with us, Robin," people said.

But always he answered no.

"Then, come back some day."

And he answered maybe. And next day he went on through the snow, on towards the mountains in the south.

Winter was almost done when he crossed the mountains. He climbed and clambered and slipped and slid on rocks covered with ice like glass. Often he was in danger of his life. But a clear eye and a sure foot and a little luck saved him time and again.

As for giants, he saw none of them. They must have slept right through the winter. Sometimes in the night he heard a rumble through the earth, as though someone was snoring far away.

The first time he heard it, he woke. The second time he looked about him. But the third time, he lay down and went to sleep again. And in the morning all was still.

So he came down from the hills on to the plain. He was in another land. But there were still farms by the road and mills by the stream and people working for their living.

They looked at him strangely as he went past, swinging his staff and whistling. The dogs ran out but when they saw him they ran in again and left him alone.

There was little work on the farms and less food. There was not much for the farmers and their families, let alone a traveller who told strange and wonderful tales.

Still Robin kept going, moving always to the south. Meg had told him to travel till he found his journey's end and he knew it was not yet come.

One day he came to a town set on a hill. Round it was a river and above it sat a castle with tall thick walls, dark against the sky.

It was late and he was footsore and hungry as he trudged through the market place. Now it was empty, the stalls were all stacked away, the ground was bare. No boys were to be seen, not even dogs hunting for scraps.

The sun had hidden behind the castle walls as he passed a blacksmith's forge. Inside, the fire still blazed. There was the clink of iron as the smith worked. Robin saw him swing his hammer in the air and bring it down.

Then he stopped. For on the other side of the fire, sleeves rolled up, holding the white hot metal in a long pair of tongs, was a bright-eyed girl, her hair as red as the flames. She saw Robin and called: "What are you staring at, lad? Have you never seen a woman work?"

Robin looked away and moved on. The girl called again but he did not hear. He was tired and wanted to rest.

He was in luck, for just round the corner was a stable. He heard horses behind the door, trampling and snorting gently in the dusk. And at the side was a ladder leading to a round hole in the wall.

In a minute Robin was up the ladder, through the bay and into the loft. There he found great piles of hay and straw. In the corner it was warm and still.

Hungry as he was, he lay down, covered himself with hay and was soon off to sleep with the quiet sounds of the horses and the chinking of the blacksmith's hammer in his ears.

When he woke again, the sun shone right into his eyes. Close by he heard a low clucking sound. A hen was moving round amid the hay. Robin got up and the hen ran cackling away with a flurry of wings, fluttering down through an open trap in the floor.

Hens mean eggs. Eggs mean breakfast, thought Robin. He hunted round the walls of the loft until, low down beneath a beam, he found a little round place where the hay was pressed down and littered with feathers. There were four brown eggs still warm.

Robin thought to himself, "Will the old hen miss two? Well, perhaps one." He knelt down and picked one up.

But just as he did his wrist was seized from behind. He turned and jerked but his arm was still held strongly. There beside him on her knees was the blacksmith's daughter, green eyes sparkling.

"Ah, caught you, you rogue, robbing the poor old hen, eh?"

Robin felt foolish. He could snatch the egg and run. But he knew the girl would not let go easily.

He bowed his head. "Forgive me, mistress," he said humbly. "I was hungry. It's two days since I dined and that was on cold turnip."

She burst out laughing.

"Mistress! You are a rogue. You are the lad who passed the forge last night. Where have you come from?"

"From beyond the hills to the north," said Robin.

"Liar. No one comes from there. The giants take them."

"It's true," said Robin. "I heard them snore in the night. It made the earth rattle."

She laughed again.

"You tell a good tale. What do they call you?"

"Robin."

"Well, Robin. I am Kate. The blacksmith is my father. Come and take breakfast with us and tell us your story for payment. Then, if you like, when you've eaten you can travel on. Come, you shall have eggs."

Robin grinned, and went down with Kate for breakfast. He knew he would not travel on. This was his journey's end.

Paddington At Large by Michael Bond

Paddington helps his neighbour in the garden; he makes toffee (ending up in hospital); and he appears on a TV quiz programme. In fact, Paddington is a bear of many talents!

Paddington Goes to Town by Michael Bond

Paddington becomes a waiter in this, the eighth book in the Paddington Library. As usual he manages to extricate himself from a variety of extraordinary situations with his customary good luck and aplomb.

Paddington Marches On by Michael Bond

Paddington has always had a special talent for trouble! Read about Paddington sweeping Mr and Mrs Brown's chimney, his special Mystery tour with Mr Gruber, and how he saves the day at a charity cricket match.

Paddington on Top by Michael Bond

Paddington starts school — and the outcome is as funny as you'd expect! Aunt Lucy pays him a fleeting visit from Darkest Peru, and Paddington tries his paw at waterskiing, with the most unusual result!

All at £2.25

Josie Smith by Magdalen Nabb

Josie Smith lives with her mum in an industrial town; she is a resourceful, independent little girl who always does what she thinks best, but often lands herself in trouble.

Josie Smith at the Seaside
by Magdalen Nabb

Josie Smith makes friends with a girl called Rosie Margaret; with the donkey, Susie; and with a big friendly dog called Jimmie, who swims off with Josie Smith's new bucket.

Josie Smith at School by Magdalen Nabb

More muddles and misunderstandings for Josie Smith. She is horribly late for lessons when she tries to get a present for her new teacher. And then she helps her new friend to write a story and completely forgets to do her own homework!

Josie Smith and Eileen by Magdalen Nabb

Josie Smith doesn't always like Eileen because Eileen has things that Josie Smith longs for – a birthday party, a bride doll, and the chance to be a bridesmaid in a long shiny pink frock. But Josie is happy in the end.

You can see Josie Smith in the Granada TV serial, *Josie Smith*.

All at £2.75

Simon and the Witch
by Margaret Stuart Barry

Simon's friend, the witch, is loud and outrageous and has a mean-looking cat called George. As she causes confusion at every turn, Simon discovers that with the witch for a friend, life is never dull.

The Witch VIP by Margaret Stuart Barry

There's only one thing Simon can be sure of when the witch is around — there'll be trouble! And 'there's plenty of it when the Witch decides she'd like to try her hand at teaching — at Simon's school!

The Witch and the Holiday Club
by Margaret Stuart Barry

Simon and his friends discover a smashing café where the ice cream is the best in town. But Lady Fox-Custard doesn't approve, and tries to start a holiday club for "nice" children. Fortunately the Witch has some tricks up her sleeve.

Simon and the Witch In School
by Margaret Stuart Barry

When the Witch discovers she has lost her magic touch, her best friend Simon has the answer: "You'll just have to come to school and learn to read." But, once in the classroom, the Witch is too busy causing chaos to learn much.

All at £2.99

Carrot Top by Nigel Gray
£2.99

Carrot Top! That's what all the kids call Melinda, a little girl with a bright personality and bright red hair to match. And whether it's helping Dad with the wallpapering, playing with her friends or celebrating her birthday, every day is a new adventure.

Operation Pedal Paw by Trevor Harvey
£2.50

Andrew and his friend Warren are determined to find Andrew's stolen bike – and five rabbits which have also mysteriously disappeared. But Andrew steals back the wrong rabbits, with disastrous consequences!

Speedy Fred by Josephine Haworth
£2.99

Fred doesn't like staying with his grandfather in the country, and he's terrified of Uncle Joe's horse, Black Bob. And when Grandad's bike runs out of petrol and they're stuck on the moor, guess who has to ride and get help?

Dangleboots by Dennis Hamley
£2.99

Dangleboots – that's what everyone on the football team calls Andy Matthews, because he's so useless. Until the day he buys the little dangling football boots off a market stall, and suddenly things start to go right. It's great at first, but then peculiar and rather frightening things begin to happen...

The Witch on Holiday
by Margaret Stuart Barry
£2.99

The Witch is enormously disgusted; this school camping holiday is definitely the rottenest, most boring holiday she's ever been on. Her attempts to liven it up are disastrous, but Simon is still glad she is his friend.

The Witch of Monopoly Manor
by Margaret Stuart Barry
£2.99

"I feel like a duchess!" The Witch has moved into Monopoly Manor and is living the high life, but her neighbour, Lady Fox-Custard, does not approve, and does her best to get rid of the Witch.

Hey, Robin! by Robert Leeson
£2.50

Robin wants to be brave and strong, but he isn't — until something unexpected happens and he finds himself on a long and perilous journey.

The Reversible Giant by Robert Leeson
£2.99

Even with the King's daughter and half the kingdom as a prize, nobody will tackle the giant, except a kitchen boy and his friend Kate.

A Bear Called Paddington
by Michael Bond
£2.99

Meet London's most famous marmalade-eating, duffel-coated bear! Paddington's remarkable adventures with Mr and Mrs Brown have become legends.

More About Paddington by Michael Bond
£2.25

Once again Paddington's flair for landing himself in hilarious situations is evident. He decides to become a detective, tries a spot of home decorating and helps the Brown family have a *very* memorable bonfire night!

Paddington at Work by Michael Bond
£2.25

Paddington is on his way back to England after visiting his Aunt Lucy in Peru, and in these amusing stories he soon shows that he has lost none of his talent for turning the simplest situation into utter confusion.

Paddington Abroad by Michael Bond
£2.25

All Paddington admirers will enjoy reading about his adventures on holiday in France in this, the fourth book in the Paddington Library.

The Demon Bike Rider by Robert Leeson
£2.25
There was a ghost on Barker's Bonk: a horned
demon that made a terrible howling noise as it
glided along in the dusk — on a bicycle. Mike and
friends thought the bike-riding ghost could only be
a joke until they saw and heard it; then suddenly
they were running so fast there was no time to
laugh.

Challenge in the Dark by Robert Leeson
£2.50
His first week at the new school is a challenge for
Mike Baxter — not least when he makes an enemy of
Steven Taylor and his bullying older brother,
Spotty Sam. But the dare that both accept, of
staying in the cold, dark silence of a disused
underground shelter, leads to an unexpected
friendship.

Wheel of Danger by Robert Leeson
£2.25
When Mike and his friends discover a disused mill
out on the moors, it offers an exciting challenge:
to get the water wheel working again. But the
summer holiday adventure turns to danger when
the mill race floods — and three of the children are
trapped in the wheel house, with the water rising
fast...

All these books are available at your local bookshop or newsagent, or can be ordered from the publishers.

To order direct from the publishers just tick the titles you want and fill in the form below:

Name _____

Address _____

_____

Send to: Collins Children's Cash Sales
         PO Box 11
         Falmouth
         Cornwall
         TR10 9EN

Please enclose a cheque or postal order or debit my Visa/Access –

Credit card no:

Expiry date:

Signature:

– to the value of the cover price plus:

UK: 80p for the first book, and 20p per copy for each additional book ordered to a maximum charge of £2.00.

BFPO: 80p for the first book, and 20p per copy for each additional book.

Overseas and Eire: £1.50 for the first book, £1.00 for the second book, thereafter 30p per book.

Young Lions